DAVID RIX

A SUITE IN FOUR WINDOWS

In homage to *Black Angels: Thirteen Images from the Dark Lands* by George Crumb

Snuggly Slim no. 1

THIS IS A SNUGGLY BOOK

ISBN: 978-1-943813-03-2

"OKAY—so what the hell is this?"

To the peril of everyone's drinks, Carrie spun the music score round on the table as though hoping it might make more sense sideways. It was a massive booklet— not much smaller than the table itself—and maybe her bewildered expression was justified because the traces on those pages looked less like music and more like some kind of abstract art—fragmented, fractured, surreal.

"This is a music course," Terry said with a rather sour grin, running his finger round the rim of his glass as though hoping a tone would sound. "What's wrong with a bit of seventies experimentalism?"

Carrie gave him a defiant look, then stared at the score again. There was a CD of it as well that they had been given, but this didn't reveal much either. *Black Angels*, it was called. By George Crumb. Subtitled *Thirteen Images from the Dark Lands for Electric String Quartet*. This was what might generally have been called 'modern classical', though the nineteen-seventies hardly seemed very modern—indeed, in some other areas of art it might have been called downright retro.

Carrie frowned and rubbed at her face. "Gawd sake, it's too fucking hot for this."

"Hottest night of the year so far," Tom said, glancing at his smart phone. "Over twenty-two degrees tonight— looks like."

Terry glanced at him with barely concealed dislike before staring hard at his drink again. It was a vodka and cranberry juice with lots of ice, and right then it might have been more useful poured over his head.

"Great," Carrie muttered. "Pickled brains, pickled music, pickled musicians, pickled fucking string quartets . . ."

Sweat drenched the lot of them and everyone seemed fed up now. Carrie's shirt looked clammy and clinging—wet patches standing out inelegantly down her back. Kate looked uncomfortable in her skin, sitting hunched and occasionally rubbing at her forehead. Twice Tom had tried to put an arm round her shoulders, only to be shrugged off again—more of a subconscious act than an aggressive one. Terry looked nothing short of miserable, though that was not unusual for him. Mix looked the least bothered, stoically careless of the fluid that was secreting out of his face and plastering his hair and small pointed beard. The heat was only being turbocharged by the narrow space they were in and the many human bodies that clamoured around. This place had once been a brick-lined arch running beneath at least six railway tracks and it was now minimally converted into a brick-lined bar with serried ranks of tables—not unlike a train carriage itself in layout. With her usual brand of creativity, Carrie always called the place 'Satan's Vagina'. Terry just called it 'The Hole'. None of them liked it very much, but this was where students went and sometimes one ended up following the crowd.

Every so often, a deep earth-shaking rumble would fill the world as a train pulled slowly overhead, crawling towards the terminus or powering its way off to parts unknown.

"Might have storms too," Tom continued, still studying his phone.

No one responded to that and Carrie drained her glass of orange and lemonade. Tom rubbed Kate's shoulder again, and again she ducked away like a cat—an embarrassed smile and a tug at her damp clothes. Silently apologising for being haphephobic.

"You okay, Terry?" Mix asked.

He gave a weary grunt.

"Yeah, fine," he lied. "This heat is killing me, that's all."

"It's killing all of us," Carrie said with a frown.

"I know that," he responded with unusual snappishness. "I am fully aware that I have a roughly similar physiological makeup to the rest of you."

Carrie gave him a startled look and Mix gently raised his hands in a pacifying gesture.

"Maybe we should get out of here and cool off," he said with a small smile. "These drinks are being totally cancelled out by this . . . this . . ."

"This wet and sticky tube of death?" Carrie finished.

"Um—yeah."

The silence that followed that thought was cut again as a train passed overhead. If you looked closely, you could see the faintest ripples spreading across the surface of the remaining drinks as the place shook. Around them, sweaty bodies seethed, all trying to get out of the way of everyone else and all on top of each other. The harried bar staff looked as if they were on the verge of a spree killing—just a few drops of sweat away.

"Oh yes—please let's get out of here and back to the haunted house," Kate said. "I really need a shower otherwise I'm going to die."

"Really?" Carrie demanded sardonically. "Don't forget to invite me to the funeral."

"You know what I fucking mean. I'm starting to feel as though I just climbed out of a swamp."

Mix downed the last of his gin and tonic and waved at the huge score with a grin. "And anyway—if we need to analyse this thing, then we should probably get on with it."

The train-rumble faded away, disappearing back below the eternal sound of chattering voices, each trying to make themselves heard above the rest and each drowning out everyone else.

"Alright, let's get out of here," Carrie said, shoving the huge score back in her bag and standing up abruptly.

Part 1
Basement. Terry
Night of the Electric Insects

THE view from the window was a concrete wall two feet away. **GREY**. Living down there with just that narrow crack letting light between pavement and building ought to have been claustrophobic, but Terry had discovered he rather liked it. Sitting in his window seat, he could look up, out of this crack in the ground. He could watch people passing but not much else—a curious low-level and focussed perspective on London. Staring up at such a steep angle occupied that poetical realm somewhere between peepshow and washed out edgy photography—the sort of thing you might see in an underground exhibition or outsider artist's hidden folders. It seemed to catch people unawares since nearly all of a person's style and personality was directed sideways. From down below, you couldn't see much of the fancy hairstyles, facial hair or gaudy makeup—not much of the posturing and walls people erect against the world.

There was a patter of footsteps across the ceiling. Kate's lighter tread, moving from the kitchen towards the bathroom. He glanced up with a frown, focussing on the unlit lightbulb above. In his head, he could see her drifting across the room—a slight figure with her gentle, almost timid way of walking. The sound of her footsteps travelled with scientific precision down through the carpeted floor, down through the wood beams and straight into the wire that supported his lightbulb. The glass globe then radiated the sound into the room like a childish cartoon of a radio mast—expanding concentric circles that never ran out of stories to tell.

Southwest. Movement. Bathroom door. Fan.

The footsteps returned. Out of the bathroom—into the kitchen—then back into the bedroom. Tom would be somewhere around as well of course, with his heavy stupid tread. Always around . . .

Terry looked away and sighed. It was very hard indeed to be in love with one half of a couple who lived directly overhead—whose life was almost entirely transmitted downwards as audio signals. He glanced across at the table for a moment, meeting the gaze of the eyeless face of Teeth, his large crystal-lined half-geode. Thin gums of wine-red and sky-blue agate holding a perfect jagged mouth of quartz. It looked as though it could inflict a painful bite if it wanted to.

"Anything?" he murmured.

Nothing. His eyes slowly slid back to the window again. Today, in spite of the heat that sat over the city like a huge pillow, there was an energy in the air—a yellowish hazy tint to the small slot of sky that he could see. No breeze moved and the smells of the city were strong—a dull round scent that made him simultaneously thrill and cringe. It was stifling, but at least heat rises, he thought. And here was another quasi-scientific vision in his head: his own heat rising up through the building. Again it was formulated like a childish diagram—heat conduction, the house slowly flushing into hot colours as the temperature climbed. First to Kate, still moving overhead—then to

Mix—and finally to Carrie, with poor Carrie getting the full force of it in the converted attic. Without a doubt, Carrie was glowing orange.

BROWN. GREY. RED.

From above came another creak and shift—the sound of their cheap wooden bedframe as someone lay down. The lightbulb flashed an alert: *Northwest. Bedroom.* None of this should have mattered, but even so, he found himself clenching painfully in response—a pressure of mingled jealousy and bitterness that he hardly bothered to analyse any more. He stood for a moment, staring up at the lightbulb, then gave a sharp and very unpleasant laugh and forced himself across to his desk where the huge musical score waited. Heat or not, it would actually be quite comforting to dive into something as technical and cerebral as musical analysis.

"Fuck you both," he said loudly and with a theatrical lift of the head. "I have work to do. Excuse me, Teeth."

He pushed the geode and various other items of clutter out of the way and spread the George Crumb score out before him. It was described as for electrically amplified string quartet, but the score also listed wine glasses, glass rods, thimbles, paperclips, maracas, gongs and shouting/ whispering voices etc., all played by the same four players—the extended techniques and sound worlds of this so-called 'modern' music that takes what a musician can do to the absolute limit.

Night of the Electric insects—Sounds of Bones and Flutes— Devil-Music—Danse Macabre . . .

Yes—it was good to concentrate. It was good to try and penetrate the dense network of extended notation that was almost an artwork in itself. Unlike most scores, this one just seemed to be laid out like a collage, with snippets of stave included wherever they were needed, even linked together with arrows indicating 'play this now'. Even branching off one another. Staves would be reduced to single lines or vanish completely when not needed—notes with no defined pitch or very carefully defined microtones—strange symbols that were part of the language of the score that would need to be learned, such as diagonal lines, X-shaped noteheads, harmonics, accents, pedal tones. . . . The first page seemed to consist entirely of harsh and crowded tremolo, marked out not with bars and a time signature but with what were presumably durations in seconds. Seven seconds and divisions of seven seconds predominating. Presumably this indicated an absence of any kind of normal beat to it, in spite of its precise timing.

For Terry, there was something deeply beautiful about the intricacy—the sheer skill and precision it spoke of, both for the performers and in the score itself. It was a cold beauty, but maybe the cold beauties were the most powerful of all.

"Very well, ladies and gentlemen," he said with a smile. "Let the performance begin."

He shoved the CD into the computer drive, only hesitating a second at an exceptionally loud bump from upstairs. The media player muddled through its splash screen and opened. *Black Angels*, it read. Track One—*Night of the Electric Insects*. Then the music came and Terry flinched. It was indeed a continuous stream of notes without any kind of accented beat, but the sound that came out of the computer speakers was more than just notes. It sounded like a million demonic crickets. The electric insects alternated loud and soft, screeching and whispering—seven seconds deafening, three seconds barely audible, then four seconds loud again, seven seconds quiet. And Terry simply stared.

As the music faded with the end of the first movement, he stopped the player again and sat back, heart beating fast. There were still twelve movements to go, but that music had caused an unexpectedly strong reaction. His skin felt clammy and even cold—as though those electric insects were still crawling all over him.

He realised that Kate and Tom had fallen silent as well. He glanced up at the ceiling again—at the lightbulb. Hoping for a report. But there was none.

"Woah," he muttered with a half-smile. **BLACK. SILVER. RED.** He got to his feet, picked up Teeth and crossed to the window—and the city somehow looked different now. Outside, the dark evening sky was only darker, the hazy air smokier and the heat heavier. The city-smells drifting through the open window stronger. A few people were passing by as usual and Terry sat down in the window seat, filled with a leaden misery. He briefly tried to fight it, tried to push it away, but it hardly seemed worth the effort. Instead, he ran his fingers over the smooth stone—the flat polished face of brownish rock, agate and perfect sharp crystals that made up Teeth's mouth. The sticky label on the rough back read *Dugway Geode, Utah*, but that meant little to him, save for its vague suggestion of American deserts. More importantly, Teeth was heavy, solid and real.

"Fuck this."

Overhead the footsteps resumed and he stared up piercingly, as though trying to burn right through the floor into the midst of their cloying connubial mush. It was his tread this time—tracing that same old path towards the bathroom.

"I really can't cope with this, you know, Teeth?" he said. "How did I get into this stupid situation?"

He stared down into the geode's eyeless face. The mouth of crystals sat painfully under what might have been a vague nose and forehead, all marked out in different colours of rock—but no eyes. It looked aggressive—almost frightening in its blindness. But Terry knew that it wasn't. Sometimes a chunk of rock was the most comforting thing in the world.

GO, Teeth said—hard, cold and unmoving as it always was.

"Yeah," Terry agreed. "I should just go. Why stay here and listen to their crap?"

He stood up and helped himself to a glass of wine from a bottle on a shelf. He sipped it slowly, listening—but there were no more sounds from overhead.

"I should have just forgotten she even exists," he said with a bitter frown. "Right? But instead I had to end up living right underneath her."

He glanced at the score again. *Night of the Electric Insects.* That was what it felt like sometimes. Insects in the brain that never shut up, that could never be shaken out. Who was stupid enough to think that love was something sweet and romantic? It was an utter horror. One of the most destructive forces in the known world. And what was romance other than the collective delusion that happens when two people forget that there is anything else in the world beyond themselves? Even the dense black notes on the page seemed to fit perfectly. You could feel it, whether you read music or not. It was music that *hurt.* An unexpected blast of fellow feeling from this bit of seventies experimentalism. Paranoia, loneliness, jealousy, love . . .

He paced back to the window again and glared up at the mustard sky. Unmistakably a storm was coming. It almost felt as though the music had summoned it—radiating a charge into the atmosphere that had to be answered with lightning and thunder.

He shivered, a prickle running down his back—and then, without any fanfare, the world went blank and he woke up in a pool of red.

RED. OUT. SKY. DOWN.

These blanks happened occasionally—it was as though an emotional control slider somewhere within him was jerked up so high that the signal just burned out. It was very sudden—a sharp jolting plunge into a period devoid of time with only a vague memory of moving shapes. His eyes were wet. Soaked in fact. There had been motion— of some kind. There had been a sound in his room as well. The sound of smashing glass. For a while he had floundered helplessly, but that sound had caught his at- tention enough to allow him to focus his mind again— just a little. And now the wine bottle he had drunk from was lying around him in pieces within a spreading puddle. Had he dropped it? Or hurled it? The startled eyes of a woman staring down at him from the street above also got through for a painful moment, then she straightened up quickly and hurried on.

RED. PURPLE. CRYSTAL.

He blinked.

More bumps from overhead. In stereo this time. Both of them were moving.

Northeast, the lightbulb said. *Living room. Room light on. Fan on. Radio on. Computer on.*

"Shut up. Please."

He was getting back in control now, but he only knew one way to escape from this black abyss of emotion. He staggered to his feet, grabbing one of the larger glass shards as he went. Then one sharp edge went into his upper arm. He stared down at the line of red, at the faint older white lines that kept it company, and gave a shivery sigh. But it worked. The pain and violation grounded him somehow, brought him back to earth. He remained frozen for a moment, then he reached over and picked up Teeth. The stone hemisphere felt comfortingly heavy in his hand.

"Well, Teeth?" he asked. "Anything to say?"

Teeth was silent. Terry stared down into its eyeless face and sighed. No—there wasn't really anything to say.

But there was elsewhere, it seemed. From above. As though his own brief explosive blank had been transmitted up through ceiling, as though the lightbulb that usually radiated information had become an emotional microphone, there was a sudden burst of new sounds—sounds that his senses picked up, analysed and reached conclusions on very quickly. A bump and a bang. Then a hint of raised voices. Another bump. The sound of a door. A stumble of feet in the hall overhead. And Tom's voice outside his apartment: "Okay, okay, I'm going. Jeez!"

He couldn't make out what she said in return. Her voice sounded quiet and disturbingly rational for something he could assume wouldn't be.

The front door slammed emphatically.

"Oh boy," he said with some kind of infinite weariness. What did you have to do to get chucked out of your own house? And for him, were things like this a balm or some kind of increased horror? He drew a huge breath and let it out again—then repeated it, feeling a sense of calm flooding through him as the last tendrils of his emotional explosion faded slowly away. Don't think, he told himself. Don't analyse whether it's good or bad. Best to save that for when he was feeling stronger. Teeth said nothing, but Terry could almost imagine it nodding in agreement. He rubbed at his forehead, realising that he was literally wet with a mixture of sweat and tears. Then he examined his arm, which was also wet. Red on his skin. Red on the floor. All over the floor. Hard to tell now what was wine and what was his own blood. He lazily grabbed a tissue and dabbed at the wound, staring at it with some kind of puzzlement, as though wondering where it had come from. It took a while to staunch it, but he finally rolled his sleeve down again. Whatever language that mark on his skin was written in, it was better hidden.

As he was buttoning up a replacement shirt, there was another faint sound in the hallway above. A familiar patter of familiar footsteps. He hesitated a moment, then stood up and hesitated again.

GO, Teeth said under his hand.

"Okay, okay," he muttered and quickly opened the door.

Part 2
Ground Floor. Kate

Devil-Music, Danse Macabre

"JUST going to take a shower," she said as she followed Tom through to the living room. As she passed the window, she carefully closed the curtains to cut out the outside world, which was only feet away and at eye level. Then she hurried into the bathroom. She stared at herself in the mirror for a moment with a weary sigh, taking in her plastered hair and gleaming skin, then she tossed the robe onto a chair and sighed again. The body was such a dreary thing, she thought. You struggled with it constantly—everything it wanted to do had to be kept under control. Every intake and output. Every substance it produced, from shit to dandruff, carefully expunged from the universe. The striven-for ideal seemed more like inert plastic than flesh—and no wonder some people preferred inanimate objects for company. No wonder some people would strike up relationships with dolls or pillows or bridges. In comparison to sweat, rust was almost respectable. Somewhere, somehow, it must have been possible to find a kind of acceptance of all that messy reality without self-consciousness or revulsion, but when she was feeling honest, she knew that she had never even come close, either in herself or in anyone around her. And she probably never would.

For a moment she imagined herself curled up in bed in the embrace of cool smooth plastic—or hard metal—

twined round her with all the intimacy of love . . . then she pushed the image away and turned on the taps. In this heat, water was the most important substance in the world. Water to fight water—even to fight metal—and with strange eons even plastic would succumb. And sex with water . . .

She quickly washed herself down, letting the water carry the sweat off her body with blissful coolness, leaving her with an ethereal floaty sensation. **BLUE. GREY. YELLOW.** As she stepped out again, dripping all over the bath mat and floor tiles without shame—let the world be baptised in the magical liquid—it occurred to her that these moments after a shower were the only moments when she felt truly at ease. It was a shame they were so ephemeral.

"What the fuck's with this weather?" Tom demanded as she stepped back into the living room. He had opened the curtains again, she noticed with a flash of annoyance. She checked her robe carefully, then joined him, keeping out of view of any passers-by. **RED BRICK. BROWN. GREY.** There was no wind outside, just a dull haze that sat over London—air feeling almost like a liquid. It looked frightening, but powerful—a massive energy close by waiting to be released. People were passing only a few feet away. A few even glanced at them as they stood at the window and Kate found herself wondering what they could see of her, lace notwithstanding. Tom didn't seem to care. And everyone looked too hot, too urgent and too worried about whatever apocalyptic weather this foretold to pay much attention to her.

"I should like to fly right now," she murmured. "Way way up there where it's cooler . . ."

"I dunno if they'd let any planes up with this storm coming."

"I don't mean in a plane," she said patiently. "I mean . . ."

. . . visions of herself soaring through that motionless heavy air, naked so that her body could sweat the way it was supposed to—arms outstretched—the air curling and rippling over her—so thick it was like swimming . . .

"I mean like an angel."

He gave a tolerant laugh and she was about to try and explain more when she was interrupted by a sound—the sound of smashing glass, clearly carried in through the open window. She glanced round with a worried look. Another smash came, then a third.

"What was that?" she asked.

Tom shrugged.

"I dunno—something downstairs. With that fruitcake, anything is possible."

She gave a frown. "Remember that time he destroyed most of his kitchen?" she asked uneasily.

"Yeah," he said without much sympathy.

Kate stepped back into the bedroom, fumbling for some clean clothes. Tom followed her and she hastily slipped her trousers on and took control of her body posture again. Stand to attention you 'orrible bitch already . . .

"What do you want to do tonight?" he asked.

"I have to get on with this analysis."

"Oh—yeah," he said reluctantly. "Umm hmm—you need me to help with anything?"

"No, I'm just going to get on and nail it if I can."

"What's the assignment?"

"A bit vague—I need to listen to it. And—and—and I need to look at how the extended notation and sound world fits into the general American experimentalism of the time. Compare the techniques and musical ideas with people like John Cage who opened up sound in the 50s and 60s, etc. And also explore a bit of the background to the piece. It says here it took a year to write and it was originally about religious strife . . . and was built using numerology—seven and thirteen. And . . ."

"Uhuh. How?"

"I . . . don't really know yet. Give me a chance—I never heard it before."

She hurried back into the living room and shut the window, dragging the curtains across it again.

"Must we?" he asked.

"You know I can't relax when people can see in," she said.

"But they can't—you installed the most opaque and densely ornamented lace curtains in London."

She sighed and sat at the computer, putting the *Black Angels* CD in the drive and opening the media player. Tom settled on the sofa. She spread the score out on a chair beside her, opened an internet browser with a search engine ready to hand, opened a free word processor program to write notes and then prepared to dive in.

A deafening screech of strings rang out.

"Geez," Tom cried. "What the fuck is that?"

Kate had also flinched away from that blast of sound. On the score, the dense notes had looked aggressive and vicious, but it was another thing entirely to hear it in reality.

"*Night of the Electric Insects*," she said, over the noise.

"You what?"

"That's the name of the first part—*Night of the Electric Insects*. It's some sort of, I don't know. Something demonic. That's what it is all about—good against evil, God and the Devil."

The screaming had subsided now, replaced by a high-pitched pianissimo whining.

"Fuck's sake, can't you swat them or something?"

Kate gave a sigh and tried to blot him out. The squealing insects eventually faded away, to be replaced by a much more primal second movement, like an ancient dance around a camp fire before music had been invented. It made her want to move—though nothing like any movement she was used to.

"*Sounds of Bones and Flutes*," she said, half to herself. But this also didn't last long before it was cut through by a long crescendoing sonic slash that a glance at the score told her was a gong played with a violin bow. The primeval camp fire froze into terrified stillness. Then long ethereal tones rang out. *Lost Bells*. They were only string harmonics, but they sounded like something descending from outer space. Something alien. And if there was good versus evil here then it was by no means clear which was which. She pushed the score away and stood up—crossed to the window, opened the curtains again and stared out with a little huff of breath. Outside, the glow of the evening looked unearthly—as though the city was a massive light source that radiated an orange aura. For the moment at least, she had forgotten about avoiding the people as they passed by, almost seeming to float down the street.

BRICK SILVER. STONE GOLD.

"You okay?" Tom asked.

She blinked.

"Yeah," she said softly. "You never seen someone really listening to music before?"

"This stuff is crazy," Tom muttered and Kate felt a stab of anger. With perfect timing, there was an answering stab from the music as well, as a violin interrupted with a furious sound. It grated and shrieked in a florid solo like a classical musician on acid.

"If you don't like it, fuck off and let me get on with it," she snapped.

Tom subsided, looking guilty, and Kate returned to the score. It took her a moment to find the place, but this was the movement called *Devil-Music*.

"This is the Devil's violin," she said, as the entire quartet growled and grated obscenely—pedal tones they were called, though she had no idea how they were made. She would have to ask Mix.

"It sounds like it," he said. "Either that or indigestion."

Kate pulled a face and switched the music off, cutting out that horrendous sound. For a moment she just stared at the computer screen.

"Would you please leave and let me get on with this?" she snapped.

"Hey—I live here too you know. I'll go to the other room and leave you to it."

"No," she said, feeling as though something was clamouring around the outside of her brain, trying to get in. "There are times—and this is one of them—when I can't think when you are around making snarky remarks. Please go out for a walk or something."

"The fuck with that," he said, looking frightened. "In this weather? You can't just . . ."

"Just get out of here for gawd sake," she yelled. Then she collected herself. "Please," very politely now. "I don't want you here, okay?"

WHITE. BLUE.

He stared at her blankly, his face filled with some kind of innocent horror.

"But . . ."

She jumped up and pranced across to the door of the apartment. It felt as though her feet were following the strange jagged sounds of the Devil's violin. Devil or not, that had to be the best musical depiction of anger she had ever heard.

"Get out," she said. She wanted her voice to grate like those pedal tones, but instead it came out with that same extraordinary politeness. "Go and have a drink or something—where they play music you can analyse in two seconds." She hustled him to the door, then stood over him while he fumbled stupidly with his shoes.

"What's got into you?" he demanded, looking so much like a sulky little boy that she had to restrain herself from kicking him.

"I just need to be by myself for a bit," she said calmly. "Don't we all? I need to work. And I need a bit of breathing space." He staggered to his feet and she pushed him out of the room, following him down the hall.

"Okay, okay, I'm going," he cried. "Jeez! You really can be a spoiled brat sometimes."

She watched the front door slam after him then spun away and danced back in again and immediately pressed play.

PURPLE. BLACK.

"Yeah," she cried triumphantly, rolling the sound low in her throat, arms in the air. The *Devil-Music* continued and she stood in the middle of the room, feeling it flow through her. It had become grotesque and rhythmical now—the *Danse Macabre*—and she began to move rapidly and jerkily, flailing her arms around and twisting her body like a puppet. It was an obscene and crazy dance, with lewd gestures and jerks of her hips—far more than she had ever seen anyone do on the pornographic dance floor with its too-simple beat. It was starting to bring the sweat back too, but somehow even that didn't matter now. She quickly pranced back out of the door and into the hallway, that shadowy space of faded communal carpet and discarded pizza menus where the narrow basement stairs descended and the once-grand main stairs climbed. She danced the length of it, but even as she spun round to return, the music wound down and stopped, leaving her feeling stranded. These movements were not very long unfortunately. Whatever it was that came next was so quiet that she could hardly hear it now, but that did reveal another sound—from somewhere below her—and she glanced round to find Terry standing in his doorway in the shadowy stairwell. "Oh boy," she said with a slightly embarrassed grin. "I guess you saw some of that?"

Top floor. South-west. Bathroom light on. Living room light on.

"Yeah—you're a good dancer. You okay?"

Kate scrambled half way up the staircase that led to the upper floors and sat down on one of the steps. It was the only comfortable option in this utilitarian, uncared for hallway. "Absolutely fine," she said with an expansive gesture. Terry climbed up and sat down beside her. There was something in his hand that bumped roughly against her bare arm.

"What's that?" she asked.

"You remember Teeth?" he asked. "He's a comforting friend."

BROWN. GREY.

"Oh yeah," Kate said, taking the geode and cradling it on her lap. Its heavy weight felt obscurely satisfying and she found herself wanting to stroke it as though it were a cat.

CHILD, Teeth said.

Kate stared without moving. "Huh?"

"What's that?" Terry glanced round at her and she flinched.

"Nothing—sorry . . ."

COWARD, Teeth said.

She very carefully handed the stone back to Terry, who took it affectionately.

"Are you sure you're okay?" he asked.

"Yes," she stammered. "Gawd—I need a joint. Hang on a minute . . ."

She fumbled in her pocket and produced a pouch of tobacco and a small bag of weed.

Top floor. Bedroom light off. Living room light on. Laptop on, still feeding. Torrent download. Phone active. Movement.

"New packet—I hope it's good. Want some?"

Terry shook his head. "No thanks—not sure I can cope with that in this weather."

She rolled herself a thin paper tube. That was a half-lie, she knew. She had never seen him take a puff as long as he had been there. She suspected he just didn't trust what might be revealed if he let himself get under the influence of anything heavier than a little wine.

"Yeah," she said, lighting it. "This weather is . . ."

All of a sudden, she jumped up, exhaling a puff of smoke.

"That music makes me want to fly," she cried. "I want to be a black angel as well."

She jumped up a step or two, then spun round and extended her arms, crouching as though to fling herself right down into the hall.

"What the fuck are you doing?" Terry said, grabbing her.

Kate gave a high-pitched giggle. "It's okay, I'm not going to fall. I'm only fooling around, for gawd sake."

He still remained holding her tightly for a moment, and her awareness of that touch seemed significant. It prickled on her skin, not entirely pleasantly—as though it had completed an electrical circuit of some kind. But then the hands released her and she sat down again. She glanced at him uneasily, looking for signs of annoyance, but was relieved to see a tiny grin on his face. She stared for a moment at the closed front door ahead of them. Flying here would only send her into that with a bang like a moth on a windscreen. Or maybe she could bust right through and erupt into the street, sending shocked passers-by scattering and making newspaper headlines that nobody would ever forget.

It almost seemed worth trying.

Top floor. Phone charging. Bathroom light on.

"Am I a coward?" she asked.

Terry gave her a look, his expression suddenly wary.

"Why? For chucking him out?"

"No—I mean . . . you heard that too? I meant for . . . well . . ."

She fell silent. Both Terry and Teeth seemed to be staring at her with the same expression. There was no point continuing the question because, even though she would never get him to say it directly, the answer already seemed to be written on his face.

Top floor. Bathroom light off. Landing light on. Movement. Exit.

She wished she had kept silent—but to her relief, the awkwardness was interrupted by footsteps on the stairs above. She looked round and found Carrie standing over her.

"You listening to that crap as well?" she asked bluntly.

Terry nodded. "Yes. Very interesting piece indeed—but terrifying."

"Is it?" Kate asked in surprise.

Carrie gave a dramatic shrug. "What the fuck can I say about this thing? I have never heard anything like it in my life."

Terry looked up at her with a smile.

"Stop chattering on your phone, lie down, close your eyes and really have a listen," he said slyly. "Inspiration may come."

Carrie gave him a startled look.

"Well I . . . you can hear me talking all the way down here?"

"You can't—the lightbulb told me," he said with heavy innocence. "You have it charging up right now, I believe? Just leave it there."

Carrie looked at him through narrowed eyes.

"Okay, you're starting to creep me out."

Terry gave a sweet grin and Carrie gave him one last glare before shrugging him off. "And what's wrong with you?" she asked, turning on Kate.

"Oh," she said, "I just had a . . . bit of a row."

"With Tom? Oh that's good."

Kate blinked, trying to work out whether that was sarcasm or not. Carrie sighed and reached down a friendly hand. "Okay then—fair enough. I know what you need."

"What?"

"Upstairs. A bowl of ice cream. Now. You can share that joint with me and we can have some girl-time. Okay?"

Kate gave her a blank look, not entirely happy at being dragged around. But the first calm of the weed was already in her head now and it didn't seem worth offering any resistance.

"Ummm—okay then," she said, scrambling to her feet. She glanced back for a moment with a guilty pang and caught the weird bitter look that crossed Terry's face for a fraction of a second. She found herself wanting him to come along as well, but Carrie was already hustling her upstairs.

"I'll see you later, Terry," she called back.

"Yeah," he said with a smile.

As she climbed the stairs, she again found herself wanting to spread her wings and fly.

Top floor. Living room light on. Kitchen light on. Computer activated. Phone unplugged. Feelings of nervousness and unease. Guilt and loneliness. What should I be saying? I don't know. Movement.

GREEN. EARTH. RED. Mix never closed his curtains. He didn't care so much about privacy anyway, but on the 1ˢᵗ floor there was little need to. The windows stood open so that the evening air could sweep where it wanted. He simply stood there, letting it come. The sounds of this music reminded him of the sounds of the forest—whispers, rattles, chirps and haunting songs. It was only frightening in the way the night sounds were frightening—only frightening if you allowed yourself to be taken over by the fear of the unknown or the strange. In this dark forest of violins, viola and cello, there was something that almost spoke of home . . .

There was a knock at the door and Mix gave a light sigh, jolted out of his reverie. He called a come in.

"Oh," he said. "Are you ok? I thought I heard—something smash. The open window . . ."

"Yeah—sorry about that," Terry said. "I—um—dropped a bottle. Just ignore it."

Mix gave him what he hoped was a sympathetic look. Terry's eyes were gleaming and he looked tense and sharp. In his hand was the familiar round shape of Teeth.

"I—was wondering," he said awkwardly, "if you . . . I mean, if you have a moment to . . ."

It was clear enough what he meant—and clear to Mix that whatever remark was about to leave his mouth was going to be a lie. Terry simply needed to not be alone for a few minutes, and Mix was happy to play along. He was well aware of the trouble and chaos that sometimes ghosted Terry's mind—too many bitter and painful emotions to deal with and no levies or sea walls for protection. It was somewhat scary because Mix didn't really know what to do about it—if it was even possible to do anything. But the least you could do was try.

"I just wondered how you were getting on with the assignment?" Terry asked, glancing at the computer, which was playing through the movement called the *Sarabanda de la Muerte Oscura.*

"I haven't started," Mix said. "It's a lovely piece, but . . ." He turned back to the window, gesturing Terry to join him. Behind them, the ethereal sounds of wineglasses began ringing out. Under those long icy tones, London seemed bathed in a curious sombre tranquillity. **GOLD. GREY.** Even the light seemed to match now, as the last of the day faded into ominous yellowish streaks in the clouds. Then a quiet and eerie high-pitched melody began on solo cello.

"These wine glasses are fantastic," Mix said. "I need to get myself some of these."

"How's it done?"

Mix tapped his violin bow with a smile.

"Different amounts of liquid in each one to tune them—then play them with this. It's just fucking beautiful."

Mix reached out and paused the media player. Then he took up his own violin and tucked the chinrest under his chin.

"*God-Music,*" he said, glancing at the score. "It's a piece about war and religious conflict after all—that's why it seems to contain a battle between what you might . . .

loosely call good and evil. But of course there is no actual winner. Just as there is no actual winner in the contradictions that form us all. Make what you will of all that. I think music like this allows you to paint your own stories onto it."

"Yeah?"

"Imagine you're walking in a forest, listening to the calling insects and the strange sounds of loneliness. If you're terrified, you'll see the forest as a horror movie—you'll hear this music painting demons and devils. If you're not afraid though, the forest sounds are beautiful. They can be taken without threat. And the music likewise. You don't have to be afraid of the Devil."

There was a silence.

"I think I recognise them too easily," Terry said. "The same devils that witter inside my head." Mix gave him a sombre look. "And—I guess you're right. I am terrified. I don't think I like this woodland very much."

Mix nodded.

"Thirteen and seven," he continued at last. "Again. Five sixteen time though. I don't know what that . . . has to do with it. But everything has patterns."

He began to play the melody line on his violin. It was supposed to be for cello, but it was high enough for him to manage it. For such a modernist piece, straight out of the American experimentalism of the 60s and 70s, this was surprisingly beautiful and simple—an archaic sounding tune not composed in any familiar key. There were even a few microtones in it. Played there, in that ordinary room, and with Mix's heavy breathing as he concentrated, it didn't sound anywhere near as ethereal as it did on the CD recording—but even so, the sound rang out over the city as though he were some dark lord playing from his high tower.

"Bastard key signature though," he muttered, putting the instrument down with a grin. He started the CD again and set this one track, the *God-Music*, to loop, over and over. Then he re-joined Terry at the window and they continued staring out. "The storm is getting closer," he said. "This is a night when you tell the truth—or go crazy. Right?"

He could feel Terry's wary glance flickering over him.

"Truth or dare?" he asked with a forced smile.

"Yes," Mix said. "Or maybe not. I think . . . maybe I already know your truth. At least the important part."

Terry's glance became a stare.

"Really?"

"You ain't exactly hiding it. When you love someone, it tends to put so many tendrils into every part of your life, it takes a certain type of blindness to miss it."

There was a long silence and Mix began to wonder whether he should have kept quiet.

"Does she know?" Terry asked.

"I don't think Kate lets herself know," Mix said. "Or she pretends that she doesn't. She'd no doubt prefer to keep things simple. Some sweet world where everyone plays precisely the roles she wants them to. And who can blame her?"

More silence.

"You never told her then?" Mix asked.

"Is there any point?"

He shrugged. "Maybe."

"What do you think, Teeth?"

Silence.

"What does it say?" Mix asked, glancing at the geode and only half convinced that Terry was joking.

"It said **TELL**—but . . ."

He sadly turned away from the window—a very slight tremble visible in his hands.

"They fight all the fucking time," he said with a sudden shrill tone. "They hate each other. They have no fucking idea how to . . . what she . . ." He coughed, embarrassed. "I have no doubt he'll be back in a few hours—as usual. Crawling in. But anyway—subject closed. I don't think I have any other secrets. And there's not much I can do with that one, is there?"

"There is something safe about even a rotten relationship," Mix said. "Or one without an emotional connection. On the one hand you're not alone, on the other you're safely away from the big scary emotions. You can exist in a state almost of numbness, and it is a comforting numbness . . ."

"Your turn," Terry said woodenly and Mix sighed. Maybe Terry already knew this—there was no particular reason to believe he didn't.

"I think I'd rather a dare. But yeah—what can I do in this weather?" Mix paused a moment. "Have you ever counted how many trees there are lining the road on this street?"

"No."

"Thirteen. And how many windows does this house have at the front?"

He could feel Terry giving him a slightly dubious glance. "Seven—for our four flats. My little flat only has one. What does that mean?"

"Who knows? Maybe nothing at all," Mix said. "But it's a pattern. There are patterns everywhere. And are they also terrifying?"

"Sometimes they are. When they repeat with no cadences and you know they will go on forever."

There was a silence, which Mix awkwardly moved to fill. "All the sounds of the world," he said softly. "All the emotions of the world. Out there, you read them, listen to them, let them tell their stories, take them on their own terms and use them as you need. And the emotion may be real but the fear of that emotion is within you. That's all. Sometimes fear is just a luxury."

Terry was silent. Mix glanced at him, wondering if he was getting through—or if he needed to.

Terry simply glanced up with a half smile. He seemed to be looking at the ceiling.

"Now Carrie is playing it," he said at last.

"Is she? I can't hear . . ."

Living room to kitchen to bathroom to living room. Laptop on. Computer on. Media player on. Living room light on.

"She really should listen more. Some people just . . . don't . . . listen . . ."

Then the screech of the electric insects sounded faintly from upstairs. Mix glanced at him with a puzzled frown, but Terry remained staring upwards.

Part 4
Attic. Carrie
Night of the Electric Insects (Reprise)

KATE was already slightly stoned, Carrie realised with a certain sense of discomfort. She was standing there staring around the room with a puzzled frown on her face. Carrie plucked the joint from her fingers and sniffed it. Maybe it was the heat and the intense atmosphere, but the round planty smell of the weed seemed bitter and unappetising. She put it to her lips anyway and took a puff, then stared at the dank paper tube with a melancholy expression. There was something quite unnerving about a stoned friend—as though they were determinedly on a quest for something far removed from anything to do with you. It was almost a kind of rejection.

Her wind pipe spasmed a few times, not very happy about the smoke that was assaulting it.

"Okay," she said at last, not bothering to hide her weariness. "What happened? Tell Aunty Carrie?"

Kate gave a frown. "I don't wanna tell you," she said childishly. "I'm just a coward. That's what . . . the rock said . . ."

Carrie sighed and Kate stole the joint back again and drew on it. She coughed.

"Where's your CD?" she asked.

"Oh for—Not now. I'm trying to relax."

"No no," Kate cried. "We must." She dithered over the laptop ineffectually until Carrie sighed, reached over and opened the media player. After a moment, the electric insects screamed out yet again. Kate flopped back onto the sofa.

Carrie plucked the joint from her fingers and held it up to the light. Then she put it to her lips and drew a deep breath.

"That music—all I hear is a bunch of ponces showing off. 'Oh wow, look at all the funny noises we can make.'"

But Kate wasn't even listening. She was staring out of the window. As the house was on a gentle hillside, the view from up there reached a long way, even to the familiar landmarks of the city centre and Canary Wharf. Constellations of city lights twinkled in the gloom. And the clouds were glowing. **GREY. YELLOW.** Even Carrie felt at a loss for words at the scene, as her mind slowly drifted into relaxation under the gentle haze of the weed. A flickering light seemed to be playing over the sky—presumably lightning, though for the moment it almost seemed like burning alcohol. A faint, dull aura of flame. She stared in wonderment, then glanced at Kate, whose eyes were huge.

"Angel," Kate whispered. "It's . . . angel . . ." She staggered to her feet and almost fell towards it, but even as she did so, the light faded out.

"Kate," Carrie growled, "snap out of it."

"I played that music—and everything changed. The whole world changed. Rocks can talk. Minds can be read. I can fly . . ."

"Sit down," Carrie said with a laugh. "You can't fucking fly. And you can't be wasted yet either. Have you eaten anything recently?"

"I want . . . fly," she said with some petulance.

"Have you eaten anything?" Carrie demanded again patiently. "I'll get some ice-cream, shall I? Or you want something else? There's a few things in the fridge. Want to see? Come on Kate . . ."

Kate gave no response and Carrie felt the knot of discomfort wind tighter inside her. She always tried to remain brusque and strident—in control no matter what—but something about this exchange was starting to get under her skin. She'd never known Kate quite like this before. She reached out and tugged at her arm.

"Come on Kate . . ."

But at that point there was a tap on the door and Kate eagerly escaped and ran to open it. Carrie spread her hands in exasperation and flopped down on the sofa.

"The storm is almost here," Mix said, peering in. "Can we come and watch?"

"Come in, both of you," Carrie said expansively. "Switch the lights off if you want. Just ignore the smell— or have a puff."

The room went dark save for the citylight streaming in through the window and the glow of Carrie's Laptop. Mix and Terry joined her on the sofa. Carrie glanced at them, recognising Mix's violin and a familiar large hemispherical object.

"Do you never let that pebble out of your sight?" she demanded, not unkindly.

Terry held it up and smiled. "Teeth knows everything," he said. "Ask him something."

She took the geode and studied it.

"Looks more like a vagina dentata to me," she said, cheekily putting the stone to her face and giving the crystal crack a lewd lick.

"Tastes . . . odd," she said with a laugh. "Okay, Teeth," she asked, "should I spank Kate's arse and see if that gets her back down to earth for a while?"

YOU, Teeth said.

Carrie stared vaguely at the wall for a long moment. "Okay, Terry, you can have him back," she said. "I need another drag." Terry took the geode again, cradling it almost like an animal. She drew a deep drag on the sodden roll-up.

"What are you saying?" Kate asked with a giggle.

"Forget it."

The music had quietened now, but it seemed to Carrie that she could still hear the electric insects screeching. She wasn't sure if it was in her own head, or coming from the far distance.

"Is that yours, Mix?" she asked, listening to the faint sound.

"Oh," he said. "Yes—but I left it on loop, didn't I?"

"Not any more you didn't," Terry said with a laugh. "This is great. Everyone is playing it at the same time. It's all talking to itself . . ."

Carrie gave a sigh and turned to the window again. Light was flashing outside—the flame-like flicker among the clouds—and to her it almost seemed to be keeping time with the music—following the rise and the fall, the loud and the soft, the tension and the release.

"Hang on," Terry cried sitting down and staring up. "Lightbulb—help me out here?"

"What?" Carrie managed in confusion. "Has everyone gone crazy tonight?"

He was staring at the non-illuminated glass globe with huge eyes and an intent expression on his face.

1ˢᵗ Floor. No lights on. Computer on. Stillness. Media Player.

"Lightbulb?" he whispered. "Don't make me tramp all the way downstairs."

From yet further down below, unmistakably cutting through the now quiet music from Carrie's laptop, the screech of the electric insects came for a third time. Carrie shook her head. Deep inside her was the feeling that something here was really not as it should be—but she just couldn't find it.

"Is that mine?" Kate asked with a giggle.

"Has anyone noticed that all the windows are open?" Mix said. "I don't think we are being very good neighbours."

"I'm going to put mine on again as well," Terry said. "I can't do mine from up here—I switched the computer off at the wall. Let's have four black angels all at once."

He ran from the room and Mix shrugged and took up his violin. He leaned over Carrie's score and abruptly started trilling the electric insects sound as well. It was not in synch with any of the recordings—it wasn't even very well played—but it didn't matter. Carrie gave a wild cringe, only half joking.

"Gawd," she cried, "somebody make it stop!"

The sound filled the world—a wall of utterly varied and alien strings radiating right through the house and out into the gathering storm outside. It was a sound that almost halted thought and Carrie sat down abruptly, feeling dizzy. For a moment the whole room seemed to spin round her like gears in contramotion.

ORANGE. PURPLE.

"Oh gawd," she repeated. "Now I'm stoned. I think. Fucking great!"

Basement. South to south-east. Living room light on. Computer on. Media player. Thank you.

Kate landed on her with a massive hug, squirming face-down on top of her.

"I want to fly," she cried, flapping her arms.

"Don't do that," Carrie wailed as Kate's floundering hand caught her a hefty slap on the side of the head. She shoved Kate off and she danced away, running around the room, backwards and forwards, wherever there seemed to be space to run. Then Terry came back, breathless from four storeys, and she almost crashed into him.

"I love you Terry," she cried, grabbing him into hug and pulling him across the room.

"I wish that were true," he cried in a sing-song voice and laughed. To Carrie though, it was a nightmare. The room seemed to press in and a huge weight was settling slowly on her head. Maybe this was what that wretched piece of music was actually about. Utter fucking acid-trip insanity. Nothing more, nothing less.

"Oh gawd," she groaned.

Such bewilderment brought on by such absolutes. To me it is very confusing. All lights off. Moving. Low level flow. Activated.

A million chattering motes seemed to be swarming round her now. She could feel them poking her, clustering on her skin, pinching her arse, clamouring in her ears. Music shouldn't do this. Music shouldn't ever do this.

Then Terry was leaning over her, looking worried. His mouth moved but she wasn't sure what he said. His hand on her shoulder felt hot and prickly, as though some kind of current was running into her body. *Flow.* She staggered to her feet again and gazed round helplessly, wondering where to go to escape this pandemonium. The window looked inviting so she floated over to it and leaned out. It was almost dark now but the heat hadn't let up—the light was still flickering and shimmering across the city. And through it pricked more lights. Lighted windows— thousands of them. Millions of them. London just seemed infinite now as it braced beneath the even more infinite clouds. The music was softer again for the moment, but it still seemed to manifest black specks and flashes that darted between the buildings, half way between something alive and what might have been an optical illusion. Carrie was glad she was indoors.

Switch is thrown. Flow is directed. Anywhere—split, channelled. And all shall be fed. Simple. There are no phantoms. All lights off. All north-west.

Then Kate and Terry were at her side and she looked around. And the music could be seen mirrored in their faces. Like a physical presence—like an orbiting vortex it spun and sucked, focussing itself into sharp points that could burrow deep into the flesh—a penetration that Terry seemed to ignore, and Kate almost to relish.

"Am I an angel?" Kate asked.

"Teeth says you are," Terry said, and Carrie suddenly realised just how bleak he looked, staring out across the city. He looked like some kind of old and world-weary bird—like a crow or magpie, shabby feathers and pained face not managing to obscure his gleaming and hungry eyes. "And you've always been an angel to me."

Kate gave a beaming grin. "Then I want to flyyyyyyyyy."

She drew that last word out into an almost musical note, almost drowning out the insect whines from the CD play- er. There was a violent motion and Carrie stared in amaze- ment as a figure rushed skywards, arms outstretched, hair flowing behind. She could almost see the air parting around her to let her through, even as huge drops of rain slowly began to fall. Light glowed around her and trailed behind her as she curved away in a graceful luminous ark over the city. Then she was descending again and vanishing among the buildings. Carrie braced herself for an impact—a flash or a rumble or something—but it never came.

Behind her, below her, all around her, Crumb's electric insects continued to shriek.

"Did I see that?" she asked, almost under her breath. "Kate? Where the fuck are you?"

Terry ignored her—just remained staring out into the pattering rain. The expression on his face pierced through her doped senses and she found herself backing away against the window frame. All the emotions of that music seemed to find a central point in his face, in those old bird-like eyes—the vortex of sound spinning out like an old beaked plague mask. The chilling serenity of the *God-Music*, the terror of the insects, the rage and madness of the Devil—all at once. He stared down—all the way down to where people were running from the rain on the pavement below.

"Teeth says **FLY**," he murmured. "But I always did prefer looking upwards."

Then he was also gone.

Where Kate had sailed up in a flare of light, Terry streaked downwards in a bolt of blackness. And now the thunder came with a crack that seemed to shake the sky.

Love does not flow. Never. Missing. Out of reach. All lights off. My words are . . .

Carrie felt a nasty sound in her throat and stumbled away from the window, to where Mix was waiting to catch her. She stared up at his eyes, which looked like deep brown pools, but she couldn't say anything. A second rumble of thunder echoed dully across the city.

All the other computers in the building had fallen silent now, just leaving Carrie's laptop, from which came a final sound of ringing tones and whispering voices.

The silence hurt.

Postlude

*A*S one of the most important experimental compositions of the 70s, George Crumb's Black Angels was a ground-breaker in several respects. Not so much in terms of technique or musical language, which are part of a simple progression from earlier works such as those of Henry Cowell and John Cage, but in the sense of applying a feeling of narrative and an enigmatic and meaningful energy. In brief, George Crumb could be credited with taking the framework of American experimentalism and using it with an emotional maturity that many earlier works lacked. Crumb may be seen as one of the main examples of this kind of composer, forming a natural link between the advanced techniques of Cage and the more overt mysticism to be found on the fringes of classical experimental music—even such examples as the hypnotic minimalism of Terry Riley, the bleeding fingered improvisations of Charlemagne Palestine, or the icy drone-based voyages of La Monte Young. This may be called the second step of any radical new musical ideas, after the initial experimentalism had given them birth in theoretical and technical terms. It is to be noted however that in terms of Black Angels, this has more to do with musical language, emotional power and possibly the enigmatic and diffuse depictions of good and evil rather than the more overt numerological aspects of the work, which Crumb rather distanced himself from later. Maybe then, numerology should not take on too prominent a role in an analysis of this composition?*

BREAK. SMOOTH. WHITE. RED.

Shouting voices could be heard. Big, significant, yet mundane—as the raindrops pattered heavily on the concrete slabs. The scent of wet soil, even though there seemed little soil around there. It combined with city dirt and shattered human fluids and floated odorously in the air.